My Ocean
Coloring Book

PaRragon

Bath · New York · Cologne · Melbourne · Delhi
Hong Kong · Shenzhen · Singapore

Clown fish have stripes.

A walrus soaks up the sun.

Use your favorite colors on this sailboat.

This octopus is waving to you with all of her arms.

Say hello to the penguin.

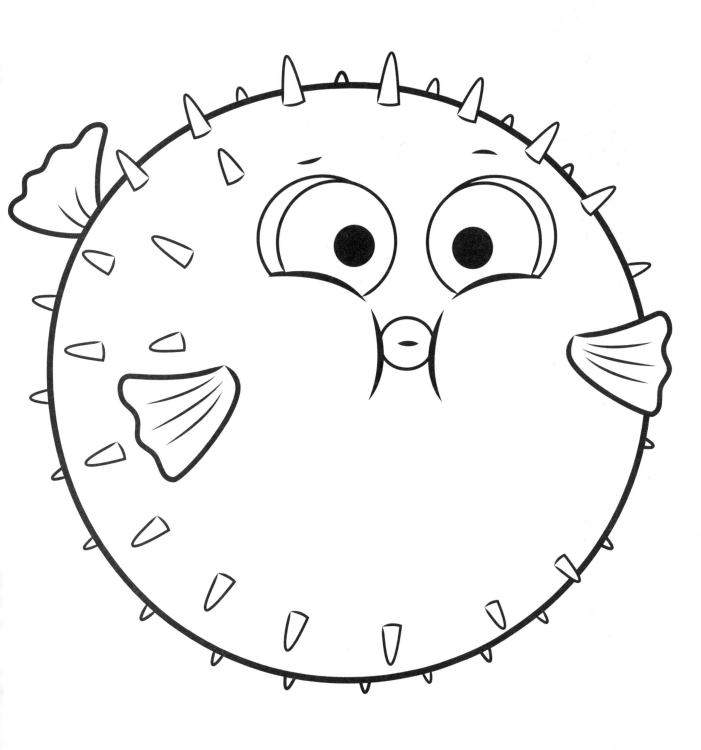

A puffer fish puffs up when he's scared.

This girl is ready for a boat ride.

Color this sea horse in bright colors.

This little crab has big claws.

A submarine moves through the ocean.

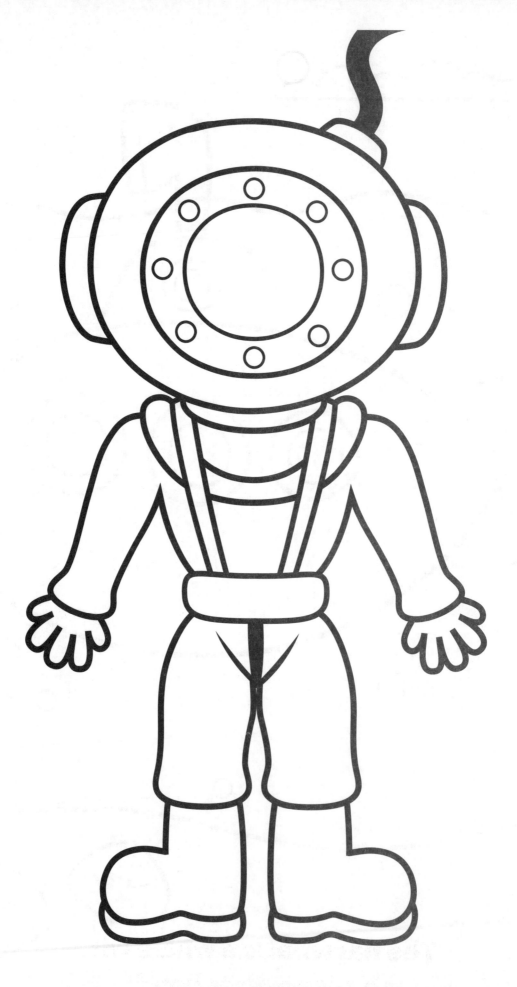

Here comes a deep-sea diver.

**The narwhal is a whale with
a tusk on her head.**

One turtle sees three shells.

A speedboat bobs in the water.

What colors should this whale be?

Look at what is at the bottom of the ocean.

Two jumping dolphins.

A sea star is shaped like a star.

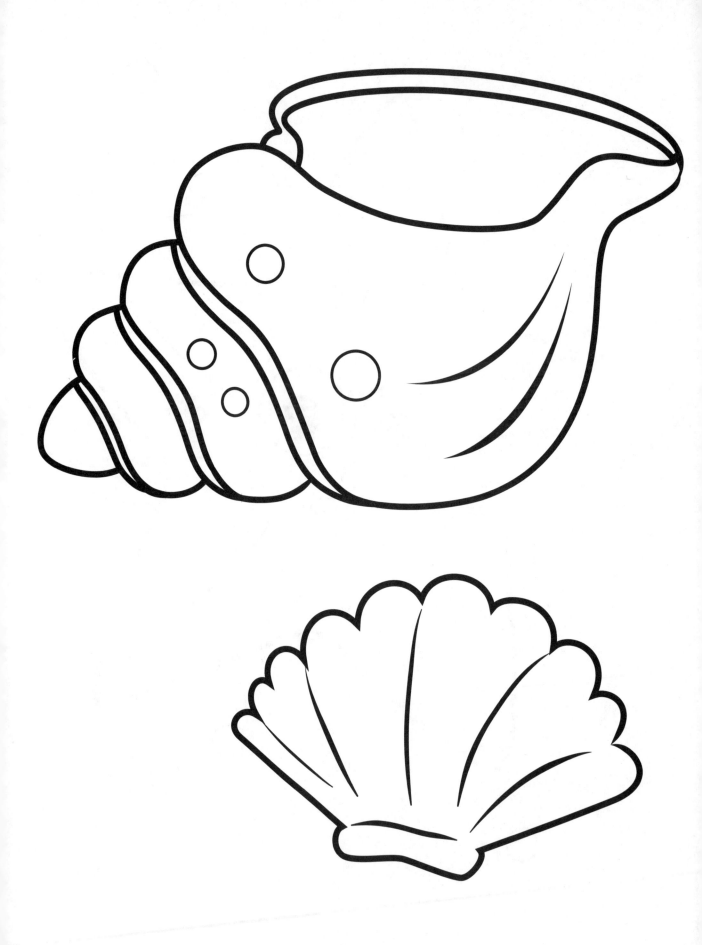

Use pretty colors on these shells.

A penguin has flippers instead of wings.

What colors do you want this shark to be?

This seal has lots of spots.

How colorful can you make this fish?

A shark usually swims alone.

Have you ever built a sand castle?

This seagull landed on a post.

Surf's up!

A whale comes up for air.

Let's catch some waves!

What colors should this turtle be?

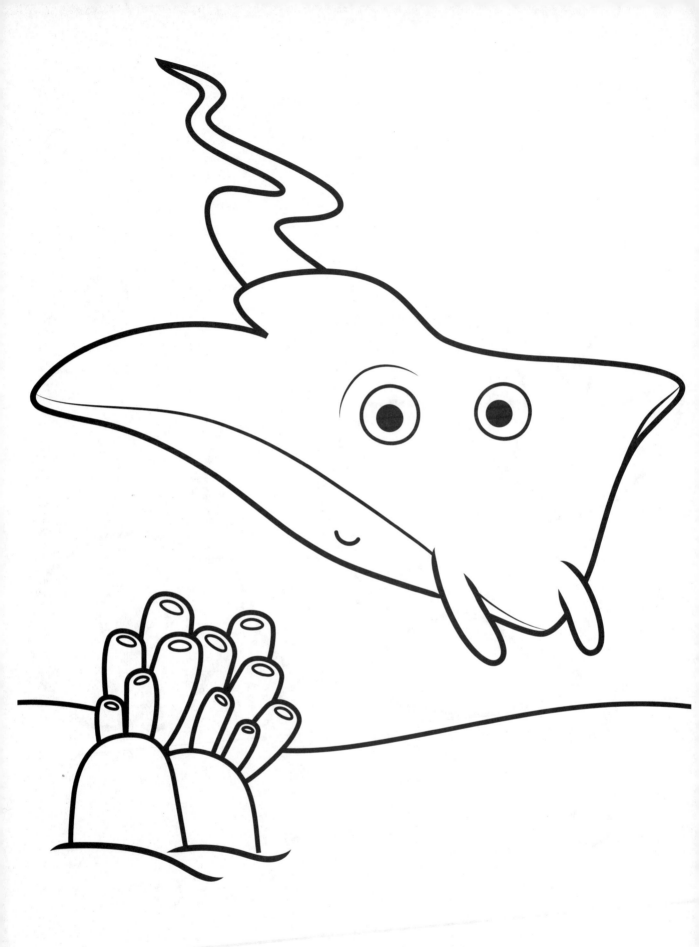

**The eagle ray fish glides
to the bottom of the ocean.**

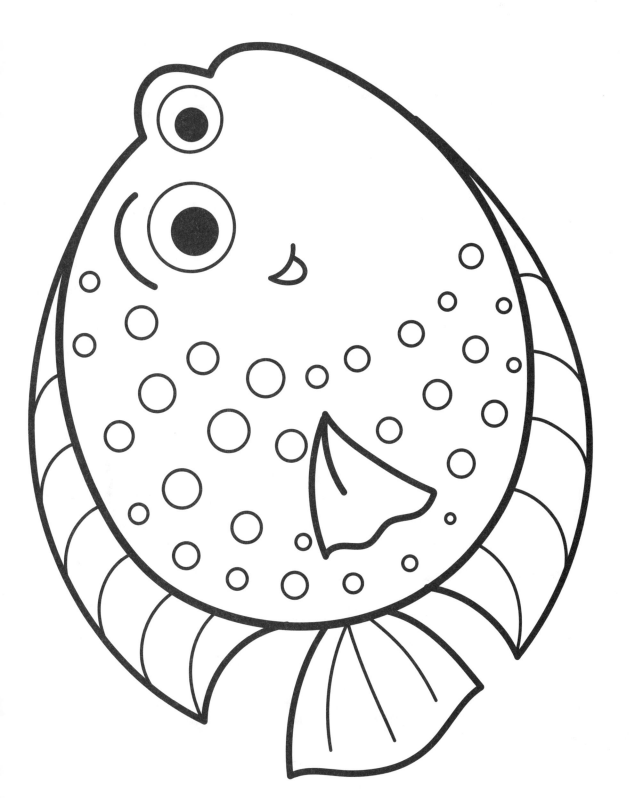

This fish is saying hello to you.

**Some people say there is treasure
at the bottom of the ocean.**

This fish is looking right at you!

A shark has a lot of teeth.

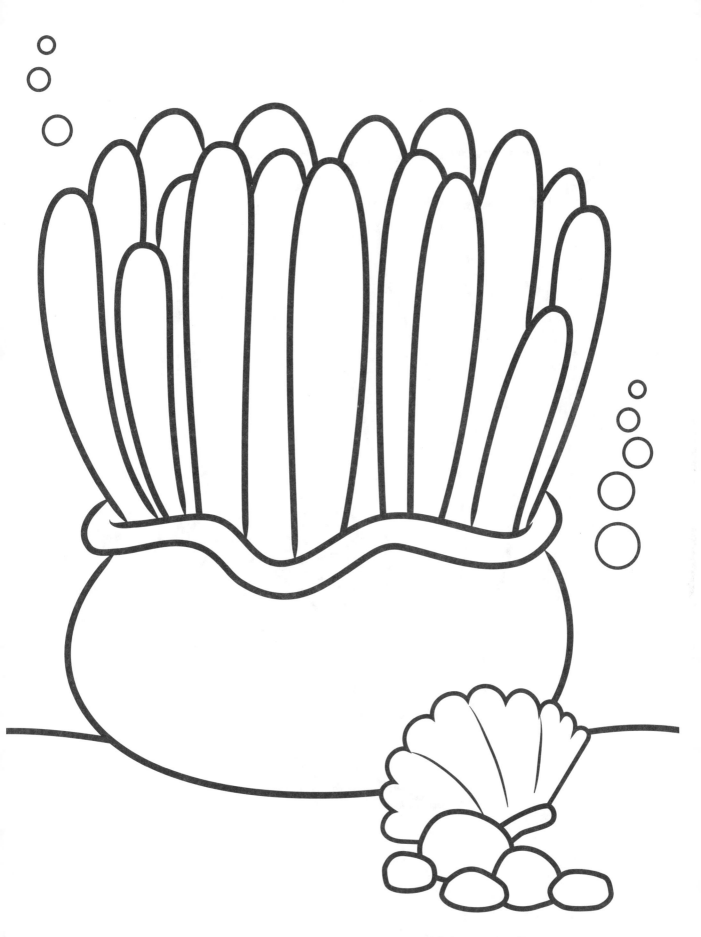

**The sea anemone looks like a plant
but it is an animal.**

What colors do you want this fish's stripes to be?

The anglerfish lives in a very dark part of the ocean and has a light on his head!

Look how high this whale has jumped.

Make each sea star a different color.

Are you ready to dig for more seashells?

**This is a jellyfish.
Color him however you wish.**

Snorkeling is a great way to see fish.

This shark is called a hammerhead because of the shape of his head.

You can see a lot from a submarine.

What a pretty fish.

An eel glides through the water.

Whales are the world's largest animals.

This sailboat needs colorful sails.

Give this squid color and more spots.

Look, it's a baby seal!

The hermit crab has a beautiful shell.

Slippery, slithery eel.

This lighthouse's light is shining.

This manatee has found some plants to eat.

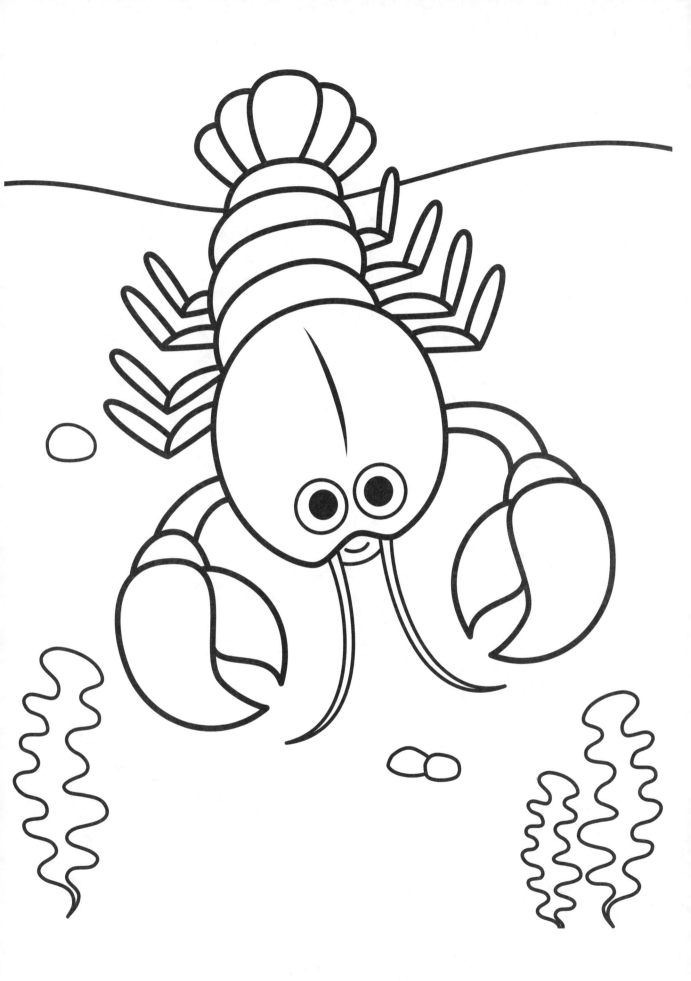

A lobster has a hard shell.

Do you like this turtle's shell?

Would you like to take a boat ride?

Three fish meet in the ocean.

Isn't this sea otter cute?

Shrimp use their little legs to swim.

A parrot fish's mouth looks a lot like a beak.

Color this crab to look silly.

A polar bear walks onto the frozen ocean.

What will this diver see?

This turtle swims toward a large shell.

What a beautiful shell!

Give this puffin a colorful beak.

A boat sets sail from the dock.

Don't they look happy to see each other?

What a whale!

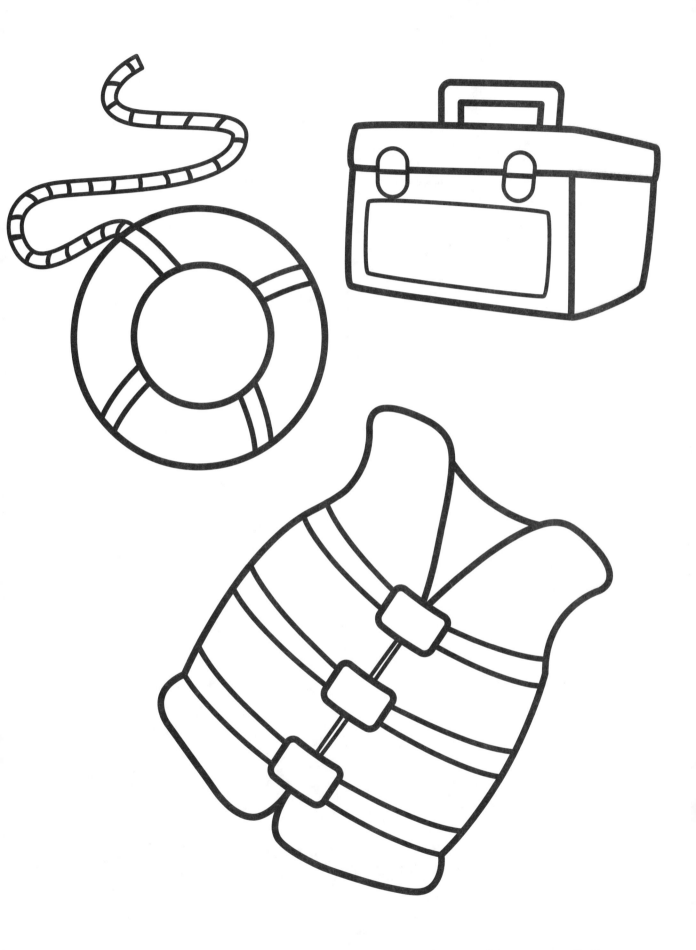

Color these things you need for a boat ride.

Jellyfish are found in every ocean.

Two ocean friends that want you to color them.

Would you like to ride in a submarine?

Look what has washed up on shore.

Some snails live in the ocean.

A dolphin jumps up to say hello to you.

Color this fish and give her some spots.

A clown fish can live in a sea anemone.

This crab looks happy on his little island.

There is so much to see in the ocean.

A seabird is getting ready to fly.

Sea horses aren't horses, they're fish!

The little boat sails smoothly on the water.

Here's a whale waving her tail.

Would you like to snorkel?

You never know who you'll meet.

A mother and baby whale swim together.

Different animals meet at the bottom of the ocean.

A narwhal and a shark swim past one another.

A seagull rests in her nest.

Some fish like to swim together.

A turtle's body is covered with a hard shell.

Thanks for visiting the ocean!